I0636560

Francia A. La Due

Beacon Fires

Francia A. La Due

Beacon Fires

ISBN/EAN: 9783337255251

Printed in Europe, USA, Canada, Australia, Japan

Cover: Foto ©Andreas Hilbeck / pixelio.de

More available books at **www.hansebooks.com**

BEACON FIRES

BEACON FIRES

NEW YORK
ELLIOTT B. PAGE & CO.
1899

Entered according to Act of Congress, in the year 1899,
in the Office of the Librarian of Congress, at Wash-
ington, by ELLIOTT B. PAGE & Co.

PREFACE

"BATHE, O disciple, thy thirsty soul in the dew of dawn," says Faust. How are we, benighted, struggling through the dank rushes of miasmic swamps, or treading the dead leaves in the dark forest — how are we to bathe in the dew of dawn until we have reached the "open" where the dawn can penetrate? Or how, ere that dawn begins to whiten, can we guide our steps by the light that shines from the mountain-tops where the beacon fires were lighted, ages and æons ago, by the elder brothers of the race?

We have caught an occasional gleam from those rare heights when our sight has scanned the distant horizon where earth and heaven seem to meet, but anon we let our eyes fall to the muddy soil beneath our feet, and are deterred either by cowardice or indolence from pressing forward to scale those sun-kissed mountain-tops; we fall back into a monotonous, vegetative existence, resigning ourselves to it even though we scornfully consider it to be only "a series of rhythmic waves of the commonplace."

Is it because the things of the spirit seem so unreal, illusionary, in this conventional and "practical" age that we do not or cannot live the life? Rather is it not because we will not permit the natural in us to raise itself up to the spiritual, and so let the spiritual be seen again as the natural? It is not that we do not know, that we have not been *taught* "the way, the truth, and the life," but because we have only analyzed metaphysical truths intellectually, have come to regard them as theoretical only,

7

and have lost faith in their practicability as applied to the ordinary affairs of life. The mind alone can never discern the inner truths; it can perceive them only by the light that shines from the heart. There comes a dark cloud of unfaith over the soul that has taught itself to *think*, that is, has converted its mind into an intellectual semi-paradise wherein it sits supreme, analyzing and classifying the fragments cast upon its shores by the sea of human life. Calm and serene it sits there, passionless and cold as the surgeon's scalpel seeking amidst the quivering nerves for the source of human pain. But,

8

sooner or later, pain seizes even that stoical soul in its relentless grasp and holds it there until in all the great universe the man sees nothing, feels nothing, knows nothing, but the grinding torment of the hell of suffering into which he has plunged. What then has become of the stoicism, the analytical research, the calm security of his self-fashioned paradise? The archangel has come and driven that soul forth from the garden of Eden, and the flaming sword suffers no man to go in and out at will. Nothing is left him but whatever amount of endurance he has gained. He has cast from him as worthless the only sceptre that could dispel the illusionary and evoke the real, *Faith* — Faith, that in the midst of torture could cry out, "Not my will, but thine, be done" — Faith, that could plainly see amidst the lurid flames of hell the beckoning finger of God. True faith is the premonition, the first faint perception, of spiritual wisdom, and it is transformed into that wisdom when the soul has learned to *feel* as well as to *think*.

To those who, rejecting the cold materialism that views only the outer husk of existence, cling to the inner life, seek for the hidden causes of things visible, and long to enter "the small old path that leads to immortality," this little book is offered in the hope that they may find help and encouragement in its pages. The writer has done little more than edit it, taking the material from a note-book in which were recorded from memory a few of the utterances of a Teacher known to many as Hilarion. Those who have read other writings of his may feel an interest in his personality, and for such the following pen-picture is given. Imagine a tall, powerfully built, athletic figure, with a frank, manly face; large, dark eyes, that from their depths seem to emit sparks of fire ; mouth rather large, with lips finely chiselled, and having in repose a gentle, almost feminine expression ; dark auburn hair, wavy, with just a touch of gold in the sunlight; strong, shapely hands, whose firm clasp conveys a sense of purity and power; a deep, full-throated voice, that yet can soften to tones of tenderest pathos. Such is the personality of this strong and great soul, whose sole purpose in life is the regeneration of the human race, championing the cause of the "common people," asserting their rights, and seeking to remedy existing abuses ; yet ever,

as a true mystic, trying to bring
all to the recognition of the realities of the inner life, and the
God within each man.

B. S.

CONTENTS

15

I

THE TURNING-POINT OF
CIVILIZATION

THE growth and development of our modern civilization may be considered as a distinct cycle, from its first beginnings in the chaotic and discordant elements of the Middle Ages in Europe to the culminating point now reached, when the added elements called into existence during centuries of intense activity and tireless progress are passing beyond control, and threaten to resolve themselves into a chaos even darker than that from which our civilization was evolved. This has been the history of each great race in the past; for, hand in hand with every effort made toward so-called civilization has gone a train of evils that was powerful enough to counterbalance any good, and which sooner or later has swamped the nation receiving those benefits. Humanity, the humanity of the nineteenth ɪ tury, stands on the edge of an abyss which, as the cycle draws to a close, perceptibly yawns to receive it ; the forces that have led mankind into its present dangerous position are coalescing and combining for its ultimate overthrow. Many of its units are in the position of a cripple without a crutch, blindfolded, and compelled to cross over a raging torrent on a single unstable plank. Scientific research has been the principal factor in upbuilding the present civilization ; and, having begun in a revolt against the senile theologies, with their nature-hating creeds, it took an ever increasing trend toward materialism. Science rejected the creeds of priestcraft, but absorbed its cant, intellectual tyranny, and selfishness. Materialistic science has done its work, and has done it well from the standpoint of those self-interested ones who, under the guise of devotion to science and humanity, have achieved distinction, and laid up for their own exclusive use all the treasures of earth their capacious hands could grasp. In their arrogance they have unhesitatingly attacked the very foundations of the Universe, have made Faith, Love, and Trust, the golden apples on the tree of life, subjects of widespread ridicule and contempt. And the masses who have ministered to their caprice, through

ignorance of their actual stand-
ing or real motives, are now
reaping the results in atheism,
nihilism, and rebellion against
God and man. Promise after
promise remains unfulfilled — for
these poor, deluded enemies of
the human race cannot see that
when they had reached the middle point of investigation they
had thrown away the very armor
and weapons necessary to their
further advancement, the Shield
of Faith, the Helmet of Peace,
the Breastplate of Righteousness
and the Sword of the Spirit.
Without these, no man, angel, or
demon can enter the spiritual
domain and wrest from its guar-

dians true knowledge and power, for these weapons are far more real, serviceable and lasting than their prototypes on earth.

Occultism has no quarrel with real scientific research. To the pure in heart, the honest, unselfish seeker, Nature opens her wonderful eyes and permits him to look into their depths, to touch, taste and handle with spiritual organs her vast treasures of wisdom and knowledge. He may not always be able to bring them forth for the scorn and scoffing of the world, but he has seen and is satisfied. To such and to those who have bridged the chasm between life and death, between death and life, and permitted many footsore pilgrims to pass over, Occultism opens wide its arms. But it would be be remiss in duty, false to its ideals of truth and devotion to humanity, were it to pass unnoticed the traitors to the cause, the murderers of souls of uncounted millions who have been led by false promises, foully inspired ambition, into a worship of the Golden Calf, far exceeding in refinement of cruelty the idolatrous sacrifices during the literal epoch of Biblical history.

Here and there throughout these masses are those who

have not permitted the light of
the spirit to be quenched, who
have bravely stood the imputa-
tion of mental degeneracy, of
extraneous growth, of a morbid
intellectualism and other like epi-
thets of scorn, who have taken
the best these so-called scien-
tists could offer and rejected the
rest; and to these has fallen a
double and triple duty, the duty
to God, themselves and their
neighbors. These know that
the river of life, fed by streams
of true Occultism and Christianity, still flows underneath the
crust of superficial knowledge;
and if they can arouse the other
units to a realization of their

own blindness and lameness, there is yet time ere the cycle closes to combine forces for resisting the final attacks of the enemies of the race, and sweep around the downward arc of the cycle into the serene waters of the Golden Age. There can be no question but friend and foe will be locked together in a deadly embrace when the sweep is made, but the possibility of its accomplishment and its glorious results should inspire the true warrior to courage unconquerable. For the real warrior now fighting the same battle on the spiritual plane of being knows — for he is Knowledge

— that he can and must win in this battle of life, or the earth be dashed into fragments that will fall upon other worlds piece by piece for ages to come.

The separation of intuition and virtue, of mind and conscience of the scientific aristocracy from the so-called herd, is the greatest calamity that can overwhelm a nation. Justice, mercy and love are ignored, or are forgotten in the turmoil of great international struggles; the result of the worldly education of the so-called cultured classes is simply a loss of sensation; they become perfectly indifferent to the fate of nation or people, and so we

must count them out in the strug-
gle. Here and there one will
cast the skin of self-gratification
aside and come out on the side
of the people; but the majority
of them will wallow in their
moral filth until they are taken
out by the neck, or succumb to
the inevitable when they find
that they can no longer defeat
the will of the people.

The lives of nearly all of us
are, as a usual thing, concerned
with events very different from
the bloody outrages, the carnage,
rapine and feuds, of the early
and middle centuries of the
present racial cycle; our natures
have become more self-repressed.

We do not laugh as we once laughed ; our tears have become silent, almost spiritual. Our heartache is not discernible by the casual observer, but is more deeply graven on our faces. As compared to a knight of the Middle Ages, we now think of a man seated upon an office stool, poring over a ledger, balancing accounts, with lines of care, anxiety, self-repressed passion, running from angle to angle of a soul-starved face; lending only an unconscious ear to eternal laws, submitting without protest to the destiny he feels creeping upon him: paresis, paralysis, mayhap, for him; charity, the streets, the poor-house, for his loved ones; and all depends upon the efforts made by that one struggling soul in a partially developed body.

We hear much of the sublimity of tradition; but alas! how superficial and material beside the silent tragedies of the nineteenth century, with its city slums, great cathedrals, towering tenements — contrasts that may well make the angels weep. The mysterious song of Infinite Life, the ominous silence of the Universal Soul, the low murmur of the eternities past, present and future, roll over us in waves as we attempt to associate our own and the lives around us with the eternal verities.

The heinous crimes that were perpetrated during past centuries under the guise of Christianity, and the black magic in the name of Jesus, nearly all of which has been primarily caused by the misuse of the power commonly understood as the power of the Holy Ghost, caused a great reaction in the minds of thinking men and women. During the era of that reaction a great danger confronted the race, a danger which happily has been averted. This was the wave of materialism, which at one time seemed liable to sweep

away all faith in divinity. Many
minds were tainted with the poison of unbelief, and the real
Christ was hidden under a
mountain of dogma and creed.
But many choice gems were dis-
interred from the buried past,
dug out of the treasures of the
ages; and with these came
a tremendous power; and the
power that led to the discovery
of these gems of philosophy held
the balances in its hand, and
when the scale tipped once
more, another factor appeared;
and this, as the future years will
show, will unite two extremes —
the idealism of the East and the
utilitarianism of the West. As

North and South, united in a common cause in the war with Spain, forgot all old differences of opinion, so the truth of the past ages and the truth of Jesus will be united by a common cause, scientific research on spiritual as well as material lines. Dogma and creed will go to the wall, and Scientific Philosophy will replace them, until its time, too, is ended, and another, a greater, takes its place.

Already the conditions have changed so greatly that a new order of things must follow politically, industrially and socially. There has come a war-cry from the inner spheres, and it behooves every soldier in the ranks of humanity to gird himself for the coming battle. That this is the *great battle* that has been prophesied for ages, no real thinker can doubt, the war between black and white, the war between good and evil. It means the overthrow of present conditions all over the world, first in America, then in the older countries, what is left of them. In the United States the proportion of citizens who are imbued with the ideas of reform is sufficiently large to ensure them a sweeping victory at the polls if they can be united on a common platform, irrespective of minor differences of opinion. If this can be done, and well done, it means that when the time comes the man will appear who will take the helm and guide the ship of state into the haven of clear waters. It means an Adept in the Presidential chair, the downfall of capitalists, an equal distribution of the necessaries of life, and the governmental control of all great industries. It means the equality of man and woman, and an equal chance for every man, woman and child in America, and, later on, in the many new possessions that will be added to the United States. It matters not that no man sufficiently great has yet appeared to the people; not till the hour strikes could he appear and demonstrate his wisdom and greatness. In reality, no man is ever great or wise of himself. He is only so by comparison. He is great in the minds of men because of the combined will of those men whose recognition of their own extremity has given the great soul his opportunity. A nation, by growth and development of its units, creates conditions, prepares the soil for the germination of true spiritual seed, and thus demands of the Good Law a leader, a king or statesman. This spiritual seed, which is a great soul seeking experience, is planted by the law within that soil created by the great need of those lesser souls ; and while the soul itself was always great because of its oneness with the Infinite, there were certain correlations on the physical and mental planes that could not be made without raising the substance of those planes out of which its vehicles for manifestation must be created, and this is accomplished by raising the keynote of its vibrations.

There has never been a time in the history of the world when each separate nation of the whole stood in such an attitude of attention and expectation. France, Russia, Germany, England and America are breathlessly watching one another, each well aware of the fact that when the true Warrior, clothed in his armor of truth, light, liberty and equality, steps into the arena of his own, or the Capitol of another of these several nations, the history of the world will be changed in the twinkling of an eye. For the trumpet will sound " To arms," and the moment be struck when the long prophesied universal war will be declared. The nations are all hanging in the balance, and a hair's breadth will turn the scale in either direction. Such momentous epochs have been seized by the great souls of the past ages. An opportunity is given for their own advance on true evolutionary lines, and they take with them the nation that has given them the opportunity by preparing conditions and demanding of the law of compensation its fulfilment. When all the desolation, the sacrifice and suffering that follow in the train of war are focussed on the physical and mental planes, the downward arc of the cycle is passed, and on the real plane of life the fruits of that suffering and sacrifice begin to manifest, and these will return with added power and potency in the new cycle for the evolving of the new humanity. The long, throbbing sigh from the heart of the great World-Mother will then have awakened a new vibration, the last expulsive pain of her travail will have changed the moan of the sufferer into a cry of joy that a child is born, a new Race, that will join with the angels of heaven in singing, "Glory to God in the highest, peace on earth, good-will toward men."

II

LEARNING TO LIVE

THE eyes of this humanity are closed as yet. It is only a glimmer, now here, now there, of the torch of truth that reaches the outer world. These glimpses are priceless, and the fact that there are those who catch them shows the great advance of the whole. Once having learned that there are in the world teachers of Occultism, Masters of Wisdom, there springs up in the breast of the man who hungers for spiritual knowledge a fervent longing to come under their personal notice, to receive their teachings. But many such aspirants mistake the force generated by the longing for the recognition of spiritual teachers for worthiness to become a disciple. Some have fancied that to attain spiritual wisdom it is necessary to forsake the world, renounce all outer activity, becoming like the mystic of the Orient, immured in some dark forest, his mind absorbed in vague reveries, ever seeking absorption into the Supreme. Such

dreamy mysticism is one extreme
of life, the feverish activity of
Western civilization the other ;
and in neither of these two extremes can the true path be
found. The character of the
Yogi of the East, vast, imagina-
tive, loving, with his constant
effort to lose himself in the
whole, must lie in the West-
wind and receive the call to
action, devotion to that whole
in its most microscopical por-
tion. The two characters, that
of the East and that of the West,
must be fused, and the dross
burned from each. If we are
to give a form, either to govern-
ment, ethics or religion, we

must become Masters of that form and not its trembling slaves, fearing that we are doing it a wrong. We must be able to transmute and absorb it into our own essence, lay the lines and send the force over these lines to and fro — in other words, become one with it. Outer work, work for this tortured, tried humanity, is necessary — more necessary than many know; for it must give the impulse to the great current that on the physical plane is lifting the world as it sweeps around the lowest arc of the cycle. But outer work is selfish and useless unless the torch of love and wisdom in the heart of each has been lighted from the great flame, the flame that burns without wick or oil. The watchers of that flame blow it in certain directions; those catch it who can, that is, those whose torches are *trimmed*. Many of us are children yet, grasping at imaginary flame, but woe be to those to whom it has been given to pass on the fire and who may have kept it for their own special purpose, whether they call that purpose work for humanity or self-aggrandizement. Thus it has ever been with those who seek ambitiously to become leaders, guides on the path their own feet have never trod, teachers of the science of life before they have learned the first elements of right living. Playing upon the selfish *tendencies* of their followers, by subtile touches of flattery, they bring them at last into abject servitude. Even the sincere and worthy student may become the prey of such false teachers, following them until he finds, as inevitably he must, that his aspirations have been travestied, his inner life desecrated.

Do not put the treasures of your inmost heart into the keeping of another human being, however high : they will come back to you freighted with the tears of those who have suffered, as you too have suffered, in order to learn there is only one sure refuge, your own soul.

Yet every failure has a lesson to teach; and even mistaken efforts are not fruitless when a true motive actuates them. But it usually happens that in any misguided attempt one injures his fellows; and we naturally learn to hate those we have wronged. Now, one of the strongest tests of true spiritual advance is to know one loves the persons one has injured most.

Jesus of Nazareth solved the great riddle of spiritual progress for the world in his words:

46

"Her sins are forgiven, for she loved much." He perfectly understood that the woman who had sinned through love held in her soul the germs of a spiritual love that would render absolute self-sacrifice, the power to *stand still* in the furnace until the dross was all burned away.

No effort for good is ever wasted. It disappears from your view, but only to fall into the world of causes, into the soil of wisdom, to be watered by love and again brought forth to bloom.

Religion is too much occupied with the fate of man after death, and concerns itself too little with our immediate life. Learn to live;

trust God for dying. The latter is his business, the first is yours. To eat, drink and sleep, to be merry or sad, is not life. Life is the intense, pulsating, vibratory acme of knowledge, truth, love, beauty and faith. Reach out and breathe it into your own soul as a famishing man reaches for bread to sustain his fainting body.

Self-abasement, false humility, is erroneously supposed by some to be an essentially religious attitude of mind. Learn to merge yourself in the whole, and from the standpoint of that whole judge your own personality. You will then find that personality to be no better, no worse than those

with whom you are closely associated; the varnish is spread more
thickly on the parts that seem
better than your associates, it
has not been well done on the
parts where you seem worse.
Could you see beneath the surface, you would find but little difference. The Good, the Godlike, lies in the *law*, the *power*,
that is raising the Son of God
from the tomb.

Do not look too far for the
thing you are seeking most earnestly. You will generally find
it close to you. The very longing has brought it. This is due
to the law of supply and demand.
Uncover the crust of the person-

ality nearest you, the one who loves you most unselfishly, and you will generally find it.

There are sterile bits of bleak wilderness in almost all lives. Sometimes we pass them in youth, sometimes later in life; but pass them at one time or another we all must, and with parched lips and weary limbs. But thanks be to God for the oasis on the other side of each barren stretch, and for the waters of life that renew our strength for another trial. To the last hour of our mortal life the memories of those terrible struggles, battles with the powers of darkness, remain with us and pass on with us into the Silence. We look back on those hours with an involuntary shiver of the heart, as we think of the sombre desolation, the isolation, the unapproachable loneliness of those great altitudes where man first comes face to face with his own soul and in his mad, unreasoning terror of its own greatness, turns about to flee away and finds that he cannot flee from himself, for he is everywhere.

Material existence is one of darkness, bleak darkness, thick and cold, and shrouded by a pall of loneliness unutterable, through which the soul, the tender nursling, blind, helpless as a little child, totters on and on in search of that sweet voice it once has heard and never can forget. Hell, aye, hell indeed, thou mystery of life! The body's anguish is a hell, but beside the anguish in the hell of its own longing that the starving soul creates, the body's hell is joy. 'Twill pass, aye, pass it must, or the soul, undying as it is, would wither in the furnace of that outer fire; and there will fall a peace, hard-won, the peace of the great brotherhood of souls. Therefore, learn to wait. Life holds no harder lesson.

The soul of man is like the soul in a tree, awaiting the death that is to give it life ; its branches swaying in the wind, its head towards heaven, its roots in miry clay. Steadily through the long years it stands, bearing the storms that sweep over it, bending toward the earth but never breaking, waiting, always waiting the woodman's axe, the turning-lathe, the careful hands of the human creator and the Master-hand that will bring it to life in harmonious rhythm; low and passionate, loud and inspiring, tones that cause a nation to weep and arouse an army to patriotism. In its earth-life, performing its natural functions in its own place, could the tree dream of its inherent possibilities? Are we any wiser as a rule? The hand of the Creator is upon us, the loose strings of our human nature are being stretched and tuned. Now here, now there, in the great workshop we catch a few notes from a nearly finished instrument; occasionally an octave of melody sweeps around the world from a few strings that have been attuned; and the Leader of the great orchestra, the Master, is still waiting, waiting, for the full number with which the pæan of universal praise may be sounded.

III

SENSATION AND CONTACT

ONE of the most important rules of Occultism is "Kill out sensation." To the ordinary man this is most difficult of comprehension, for as a rule he recognizes the fact that to kill out sensation means to kill out life, for all life is primarily contact and sensation, without which there could be no consciousness. But in the above rule, sensation means that identical mode of the same motion which connects and holds mankind to that one rate of vibration, and will not let man pass to those unexplored regions of higher motion where real life exists, but compels him through satiety to return again and again along the same well-worn paths he has traveled since the original impulse was given by which the vibration of his single differentiated life was started, until it was exhausted, and the personality sinks like a sodden leaf to the bottom of the stream. Sensation should be *used* for development, not *abused* for degeneration. Every sensation should be studied and observed from an impersonal standpoint, that is, man must compel his consciousness to stand aside from his organs of sensation and look at each of his own sensations as he might at those of another, had he the power of such analysis. All that man holds dear of pleasure or enjoyment has its counterpart or correspondence on other planes of being. These are gradually refined and purified from the dross that is always associated with the lower planes of manifestation; and when man has reached an equilibrium, an impersonal point, the lessons he has learned from his observation of those lower forms of sensation will serve to connect him with the new radiance, the new rate of vibration, by which a realization of himself as one of the conscious creative agents or powers of the Universe will dawn upon him.

No weakling, no one satiated with these lower orders of sensation, may lift the veil of Isis and take from her hands the Key to the Temple Gates. Yet it must take an epicure, in the highest sense of the term, even to realize that there are heights beyond, ready for him to scale when he shall have attained power to make the attempt.

Many students of Mysticism have taken this rule as a guide to development, and have only succeeded in damming up in their own nature currents of force that will break all boundaries when a severe testing occurs, and sweep them away into a whirlpool of mad passion, or destroy the organs of sensation in their physical bodies. No ordinary man or woman of the present day can follow this rule without grave danger, though its spirit is possible and right. Remember, I am giving no license to vice in saying this; but I *am*

pleading for *natural* life. Here
and there, like the Obelisks of
the East, the Pyramids of Egypt,
stand out the names of men who
have scaled the great heights
gained through sore travail; for,
paradoxical as it may seem, pleasure is attainable only through
pain, and *vice versâ*. These
great Souls have left, for our
guidance, milestones along the
path they have climbed; and on
one of these milestones is inscribed, in letters of fire, "Fearlessness." As long as fear can
paralyze the soul of man, struggling for higher development, so
long that soul can make no further progress. When he first

realizes the fact of those vast
heights beyond, which are strewn
with the ashes of those who have
vainly attempted to scale them,
a sense of deadly fear descends
upon him like an avalanche, and
he turns like a hunted deer, and
flies back to those lower levels
upon which he has browsed so
long that they have become barren to the gaze of his soul; or
else he stands like the pine tree
on the side of a bluff, striking
its roots deeper into the soil,
though its trunk bends and shiv-
ers with every blast of the storm.
But as he stands alone yet con-
fident in his own strength, he
finds the storm lessening little by

little, and peace like a deep-flow-
ing river will one day roll over
his soul, filling him with the consciousness of all created things.
He has taken only one step up
the ladder of life, but that step
has placed him far in advance
of his fellow-men; they can no
longer comprehend his language
or actions, and he is like one set
apart.   The sensation of fear no
longer exists for him; its vibratory tone has changed and has
become "Fearlessness."   He
has seen another of those milestones, on which is inscribed
"Action," and flinging his cloak
of purity over his shoulders, he
steps out of the shadow into the

shine of life. His eyes are no longer held, he sees the light in the eyes of the woman he loves, and knows that it shines from the pure soul within; and putting behind him the passion that has hitherto hindered both of them, he takes her by the hand and says, "We will take the next step together." The sensation of lust has been changed to pure love, and he has come face to face with his own soul. For love alone can lead to the shrine where dwells the soul of man. Love seizes Contact, and knocks at the doors of the Universe. Sensation responds and throws open these doors.

Many would-be occultists have deemed it incumbent upon themselves to decry all sensation, all emotionalism, making apparently no distinction; and they have therefore misled many students who could not reconcile such teachings with their own intuitional knowledge that sensation is life. In the very effort to follow where such presume to lead incalculable harm has resulted; for either the organs of sensation have been temporarily atrophied, or an inertia, from which no ordinary sense-perception could arouse them beyond a very limited degree, has ensued. The natural man will find a drop of poison in the *second* cup of any pleasure to which he may have been attracted; but in that poison, by careful search, he will find its antidote, and the key to the fulfilment of a higher pleasure with its corresponding pain.

"Ho, all ye that suffer, know ye that ye suffer from yourselves!" Do away with the fallacy that your pain is caused by another. The inner self, the ruler of each being, recognizes the truth that pain and weariness are as essential to growth as are their opposites; it reaches out and strikes a note of the great instrument that must respond discordantly; it flashes out a color that cannot harmonize in vibration with the others in the aura, and a sombre faded tint is apparent. It speaks a word or gives a look to some other fragment of itself, and only too often turns around on that other with a false accusation, for it cannot always see that only its own longing for sensation is the primary cause and effect of its own experiment.

IV

THE ETERNAL LOVE

THERE may come to us a day when, with head pillowed upon the breast of one we love, one that loves us, the eyes of the soul are opened for a brief moment and we catch a glimpse of the Eternal Love. We are never quite the same again. We have touched a string of the harp of love, and there is discord in all else.   Perhaps that one brief glimpse is all that is vouchsafed us in one life, but that is enough to draw us out of the beaten track of lower levels, and set our feet on the upward path that leads to eternal life. That one glimpse into the pure and serene region of the soul leaves us thenceforth like a child crying in the wilderness — but a child who knows that it has seen its Father's face, and that sometime, somewhere, there is home and peace.

Oh, the pity of it! That man, seeking, struggling, fighting for what he believes to be the realities of life, should close the only door that leads to soul-perception

—Imagination ; that he should grasp the soiled garments and cling to them with frantic energy, entirely forgetting that the true self is not the garment, is always unseen. The heart of the one you love best is unknown to you ; you take it at your own valuation, attributing to it your highest perceptions of beauty, truth, steadfastness and purity. When the outer form, the body, is laid away, the inner self remains and has suffered no change ; you do not cease loving your ideal, the soul, which is and always shall be. That soul has never declared itself to you through the senses ; still, it is the most vivid of all existing realities to the lonely one watching the deserted casket. The torn and soiled garment was not the soul, was only the outer covering it wore. The loneliest, saddest hours you will ever pass are when, from some mistaken motive, some doubt, distrust, or suspicion that you have attributed to that soul qualities it did not possess, that you have loved only an unreal creation of your own fancy, you will yourself close the door through which you caught the first glimpse of the one eternal reality — true and perfect being — and find that something has escaped from your own soul which you cannot regain — the power of idealizing, the power of loving.

Beauty, strength, purity, courage, all the qualities that inspire love, are but symbols of the realities of the indwelling soul ; the merely sensuous or emotional recognition of them, the cold intellectual appreciation accorded them, is but idolatry. Whoever aspires to know their meaning must read with the eyes of the imagination. We are more apt to be misled by the glamour of outer appearances, the semblance of the Real, than by those we often regard with distrust as imaginary, as unreal phantoms called into being by the image-making faculty of the soul. Love may seem but a glamour; yet, while love may be esteemed blind in this world, it is itself the light that illumines all worlds, making all things clear to the inner sight.

A man is more truly that which he is in the eyes of the woman who loves him, than that which he believes himself to be. He has never deceived her; the mystery is that she loves him in spite of all she finds unlovable in him, and is therefore like the Father who may grieve over the prodigal son, but runs to meet him with a kiss on his return from his wanderings. It is only a woman who can smile up into the face of the dreaded Future— but still the Father's face — with sublime unconcern. And yet how insignificant womankind appear as we see them toiling and delving about their homes. In his egotism man forgets that the love of woman points the way to the love of God. For the feminine side of the God-head is soul.

A woman never forgets the path that leads to the centre of her Being,— a man often does; but if he but whisper a word that has truly come forth from the depths of his soul, no matter how far she may have strayed

from the true life, she will re-
trace her steps along that mysterious path she has not forgotten,
and bring out of an inexhaustible
store of love a word or look as
pure as his own. For all time
her soul stands, as it were, on
the threshold, awaiting the call
of another soul.

No single action of the prin-
ciple of Love or Desire has created more discussion or been the
cause of more curiosity and imagination, than that of the kiss between mortals. It is supposed
to be purely a human function,
but that is a great mistake. The
indescribable thrill that perme-
ates the whole nature at the

touch of the lips of a loved one is the first action of the Divine Spirit-substance on matter. No physiological description, or dissection of the organs in use, gives a satisfactory reason for this; nor is it a function of passion. Passion seizes upon and uses the power — as it does every other it can grasp — for its own purpose; but it is in no sense an attribute of passion. Its genesis is of the purest, and Christians should be the last to decry or desecrate the term, as their *Bible* is full of allusions to it. The kiss of the first two pure emanations begot the first-born Son, Light; the kiss of Love and

Hope begot Faith; the kiss of Faith and Hope begot Action; for it was through the kiss that Creative Fire brought all matter into manifestation. It is feminine, and is of the soul. Through degeneration and desecration it has become a function of passion; but when pure it is generated in the soul, not in the body, of man.

For, after all, love is in reality the energizing of the universal creative force, the subtle fire that lurks in every atom of manifested life. As an element that consumes, destroys, it becomes the fiery serpent, the devouring monster of human pas-

sion.   Viewed only in this lower
phase of its workings, it is a
thing abhorrent; but let those
beware who, shrinking from the
pollution of animal lust, seal their
hearts against love and friend-
ship also, seeking refuge in cold
asceticism and selfishness; for,
sooner or later, the repressed
nature will become the prey of
lust.   Love, purified, leads to
true asceticism; stifled, it turns
to passion.   This fiery formative
force coils itself, serpent-like,
about him who rashly seeks to
escape: it draws to its centre the
struggling soul by its power of
attraction, and holds it there until the soul recognizes its own

divinity, and by the force of that divinity transforms the passion into compassion. Desire is not killed, as we understand the word. It is changed from glory to glory — that is, from the height of self-indulgence to the height of self-abnegation.

The importance of purity of mind and body should never be underestimated; yet one should use all care lest in attempting to purify his nature he should mar it or destroy it. Fine discrimination is often needed, and if one cannot employ this, he had better rely upon the spontaneous, normal processes of evolution. The *soul* of the man who leads a natural life is but little affected by his baser passions, is never defiled by them. The golden Tree of Life, whose roots rest in Hades and whose crown sweeps the heavens, puts forth its gem-like buds in storm and tempest. Its trunk is not swayed by the storms that beat upon it, but stands upright in lonely grandeur. Those buds are the first manifestations of the soul's essence, awaiting the resurrection morn, when a single gleam of spiritual fire will expand their close-set petals, unfolding in their supernal beauty these calyxes of transcendent purity and power.

V

PAIN AND SACRIFICE

IN every union there is a great mystery — the mystery of the divine Initiator, the Master, the priest who performs the ceremony of unification. This law holds good in the molecule, the star, the universe. If I kiss my brother, there are my brother, myself, and the thrill of love which sweeps through us both, which is not passion, but, ac-

cording to the degree of greatness in that brother and myself,
simply love; but a divine law
comes into operation in this apparently simple action: in the
kiss, that one thrill of love is sacrificed. If I kiss him again, it
will not be the same kiss nor the
same vibration of that force. An
old Eastern axiom has it that
pleasure and pain are equal.
This is true to some extent, but
not literally; for while pain may
be raised into joy or pleasure,
joy itself cannot be made pain,
it is only the effects of joy that
can become pain. Joy is the
positive, pain the negative. Joy
is the natural state, pain the un-

natural. It is only on the lower planes of existence that both are necessary. But on those planes pain is the more needful, for pain creates conditions for joy to manifest. Pain causes heat, fever, raises the temperature, and in those heat vibrations the lower, coarser molecules are destroyed by the creative fires ; or, rather they are changed into another, a critical state of matter, from whence comes into being on another plane by coalition with another force, also a fire, a different state of matter — one of the states that enter largely into the formation of the matter cognizable by the senses. This is one of the mysteries of pain, and only one; but *this* brings in its coadjutor, sacrifice.

There can be no differentiated life without sacrifice. The *one* must die in order that the two-in-one may come into existence. The so-called heathen, when offering sacrifices to the Gods, understood this law. Pain and sacrifice are frequently spoken of as two aspects of the one reality. This is true on the higher planes, but conveys no adequate conception of the truth on the outer planes of differentiation; for the spiritual will converts the lower aspect of pain into sacrifice by commingling with the pain, that is, by becoming one with it, giving to it and receiving from it an element which this action has called into existence; and it is this — the sweet savour — that is the real sacrifice, not the thing sacrificed, the sacrificial stone or the sacrifice.

A great mistake has been made in interpreting the Eastern teaching. Many of the so-called teachers of Occultism have taken a flying leap from the lower differentiated planes of existence to the homogeneous state of the Infinite One. While it is necessary to state this truth, and to bring a true conception of the ultimate state of all matter to the finite conception, it is still more necessary for the intermediate degrees to be accentuated, for it is on these gradations or planes that the whole of our existence is passed. When the ultimate state is reached, all individualities are merged into the One ; and it is on the lower planes that all the sacrificial rites are performed. The eternal Son is sacrificed when it enters the womb of the eternal Mother, the sacrifice of God to himself that this son may be "the first-born among many other brethren." Without this sacrifice of himself there could be no further creation. This, taking place on the highest spiritual plane at the beginning of every world-period, is repeated on every plane of existence. It extends from the Infinite to the last son of the Æon. Geometrically, it is the oblong equilateral, and is the true stone of sacrifice, for on it is laid, each in turn, every burnt-offering, that is, every sacrifice of the true seed of life by the fires, the first of which is kindled on the spiritual, the last on the animal plane. The fires referred to are not separate fires, but different aspects of the one fire, Love. God is Love, and he is also a consuming fire. The spiritual symbolism of the old phallic rites was correct. The sin of the ancients lay in the materialization of those symbolic rites under conditions that made them unnatural and evil, for they led to the lowest sensual acts, to unspeakable crimes against nature. It is in this way that all great spiritual truths have been degraded and dragged in the filth of animal passion, and as a result man has become the emasculated creature he now is.

We associate the word sacrifice almost invariably with pain and suffering, believing that in order to sacrifice we must suffer. This is not true. There is as much sacrifice of pain to joy

as of joy to pain, and the savour
of the sacrifice is just as precious,
just as holy. The trouble is, we
are very devoted to our pains
and sufferings; we hug them
close and will not let them go,
when in many cases they would
fall away from us. When we
have made what we call a sacrifice for some good work, we
unconsciously assume the position of martyrs; we pity ourselves with a great pity; we say,
in effect, to the Gods: "Just
see what I have given up, see
what I am doing for your sakes,"
— when in nine cases out of ten
the truth is that we are really
throwing aside some rubbish,

some impediment to the growth of either soul or body. Then when we fail to receive the great reward we have convinced ourselves we deserve, we cry out, "I am not recognized, my sacrifice is futile. I shall give it all up and lead as pleasant a life as possible," — and never realize that then we had made the *true* sacrifice by giving up the false, had sacrificed oneself to oneself.

Joy, true divine bliss, which is peace, comes only by giving, never from receiving, unless giver and receiver are equals; for with the majority of people there comes a selfish realization of the *power* to give, which materializes or degrades and darkens the divine right to give until it becomes a desire to receive, and that insatiable demon can never be satisfied. For with every gratification of that desire the originally pure impulse is further distorted, until finally the whole nature is turned, twisted and warped, the power to give righteously is lost forever, and grasping, selfish egotism is the result, whose forces, contracting like the twining coils of a cobra, leave the man a soulless wretch in the outer world, a human being in form, yet having no share in the spiritual heritage of humanity.

VI

THE POWER OF LITTLE THINGS

ONLY a soul that is capable of apprehending and using the minutiæ, the small details so unbearable to one class of humanity, and utilizing them as a chess-player uses his knights and pawns for the winning of a game, can by any possibility reach for and grasp the true Infinite Potency; for, first of all, it is power over little things that leads in the end to power over the great. To live on the spiritual plane means to keep oneself constantly in touch with all sweetness, all purity, all love.

The man or woman who is discourteous, unkind and selfish toward the least of the little ones of Christ, is obstructing the very Christ-currents in his own aura and making it impossible for the potency therein to manifest itself.

No truer estimate of a great soul can be made than by watching its attitude toward the small vexations of daily life, those unexpected trivial things that are capable of tearing down the walls we may have made about ourselves and leaving the soul naked in the silence that falls upon it after the stress and storm of those battering, disintegrating little worries and cares that pile up like a pathless mountain thickly covered with brambles and briers that sting and tear till the mind grows desperate in contemplation. We think of a man who goes into the desert to fight bravely with the wild beasts of his own soul, as of a hero who is worthy of the power he hopes to win. But he never will or can win unless he has first over-come the daily trials that stay his feet like a quagmire while his life is environed by a community of fellow-creatures. For he will find nothing in them that is not in his own individual nature, and it is only the clashing of causes one against the other that produces the friction between himself and his fellows.

The natural tendency of the human race to look for its object of worship, its ''holy temple,'' and the fulfilling of its sense of duty, either to the heavens or to some point distant from the individual point of vantage, is not easily understood. It is brought over from forgotten past ages when there *was a wider separation*, when man had lost his heritage and the scales of evolution had not yet turned. But all true spiritual teaching proclaims the God *within* humanity, the duties to the brother, neighbor and friend. One never finds outside of himself what is not within, and as long as there is a wrong to be righted, a sufferer to be healed and comforted, a child to be taught, or, in wider terms, any string of the harp of brotherly love to be attuned to the vibrations of universal love, lying right at your door, in the midst of your own family or your own social circle, your individual duty lies right there. If your life, your strength, your influence, were needed elsewhere, you would have found yourself elsewhere, or your circumstances so adjusted as to leave no room for doubt as to when and to whom your influence and devotion were due.

All the great epics, all the records, whether written upon parchment and piled away in the archives of ruined, deserted temples, or graven on the walls of subterranean chambers of Initiation, bear witness to the great wars — war between angels and demons, war between elements, and war between spirit and matter; unceasing, exterminating, eternal war; and whether he will or nay, man *must* take part in this warfare, must choose sides and fight to the bitter end in each of his incarnations. If he is inclined to shirk, he gains nothing; for Nature herself will force him to a bare fight for existence on the physical plane, if he has been false to his higher self and wasted those opportunities for development which would have given him power over her forces, if he has lost his place in the army of the upper spheres; and to have lost that power and place means a temporary separation between the Warrior, the real self within, and the lower personality. There is no inactivity, no cowardice, no selfishness, in the nature of the Warrior, there is only the great desire that he may win, with the certain knowledge that he cannot fail. To look for the Warrior within, the lower personality must stand in an attitude of attention. On the physical plane this is sometimes a very wearisome manœuvre; and none the less trying, when applied to the plane of soul, are these long hours of alertness, when the tired mind and body begin to long for the shallows and undulating meadows of life. But these are mirages most deceptive in their beauty and seeming peace;

for there is no peace in them for the soul, the true Warrior, and by taking off his armor and lying down to enjoy the narcotic stupor of ease, the soldier misses the true Warrior to whom he has called and for whom he has waited long. For his cry will not fall on that listening ear unless the lines of true knowledge have been laid; and in the feverish hurry of the coming fight his senses will reel and fall, confusion of friends and foes will ensue, and when the day is over his body be found upon the battle-field, devoid of all life, only an object for the carrion birds of prey to fight over. But when

he has once found or been found
by the Warrior, has become one
with him, the last vestige of in-
stability will disappear ; for then
will come a recognition of eternal
truth, a sure knowledge of the
cause and purposes of the infinite Father-love that lies just
beyond the field of battle, a living faith that no blow will be
struck amiss, no charge lost, and
that on the banner which he
carries will be inscribed, " Victory ! Victory ! Victory ! "

www.ingramcontent.com/pod-product-compliance
Lightning Source LLC
Chambersburg PA
CBHW032157010726
47493CB00008BA/2734